TAMESIDE LIBRARIES

3 8016 0202 25209

KT-407-967

Hattie's Magic Show

HAT TRICKS

A book to share from
Scallywag Press

First published in Great Britain in 2019
by Scallywag Press Ltd, 10 Sutherland Row, London SW1V 4JT

Text and illustration copyright © Satoshi Kitamura, 2019
The rights of Satoshi Kitamura to be identified as the author and illustrator
of this work have been asserted by him in accordance with the
Copyright, Designs and Patents Act, 1988

All rights reserved

Printed on FSC paper by OZGraf, Poland

001

British Library Cataloguing in Publication Data available
ISBN 978–1–912650–02–6

Hattie's Magic Show

HAT TRICKS

Satoshi Kitamura

Scallywag Press Ltd

LONDON

What is this?

It's a **rabbit** in a hat!

But it's not just *any* rabbit,
and it's not just *any* hat . . .

It's Hattie the Magician
and this is *her* hat!

So welcome, everyone,
to Hattie's magic show!

Abracadabra, katakurico...

What's in the hat?

It's a cat!

What will be next?

Abracadabra, katakurico…

What's in the hat?

It's a squirrel!

Abracadabra, katakurico...

What's in the hat?

It's a moose!

Abracadabra, katakurico...

What's in the hat?

Why, it's an elephant!

But the elephant is stuck.
Oh, oh, oh, it hurts!

One,
two,
three,

heave...

Surely, by now,
the hat is empty.

But no . . .

WoW! What's in the hat?

It's an entire jungle,
with new friends for everyone!

What a *grand finale*.

Bravo, Hattie!
Bravo, hat!